WINTER WOLF GAMES

WINTER WOLF GAMES

THE PACK MATES OF LUNAR CREST, A SHORT STORY

by

GINNA MORAN

ISBN 978-1-951314-43-9 (soft cover)
ISBN 978-1-951314-44-6 (hard cover)

This is a work of fiction. All of the characters, organizations, and events portrayed in this novel are either products of the author's imagination or are used fictitiously.

Cover design by Silver Starlight Designs
Cover images copyright Depositphotos

For Inquiries Contact:
Sunny Palms Press
9663 Santa Monica Blvd Suite 1158
Beverly Hills, CA 90210, USA
www.sunnypalmspress.com
www.GinnaMoran.com

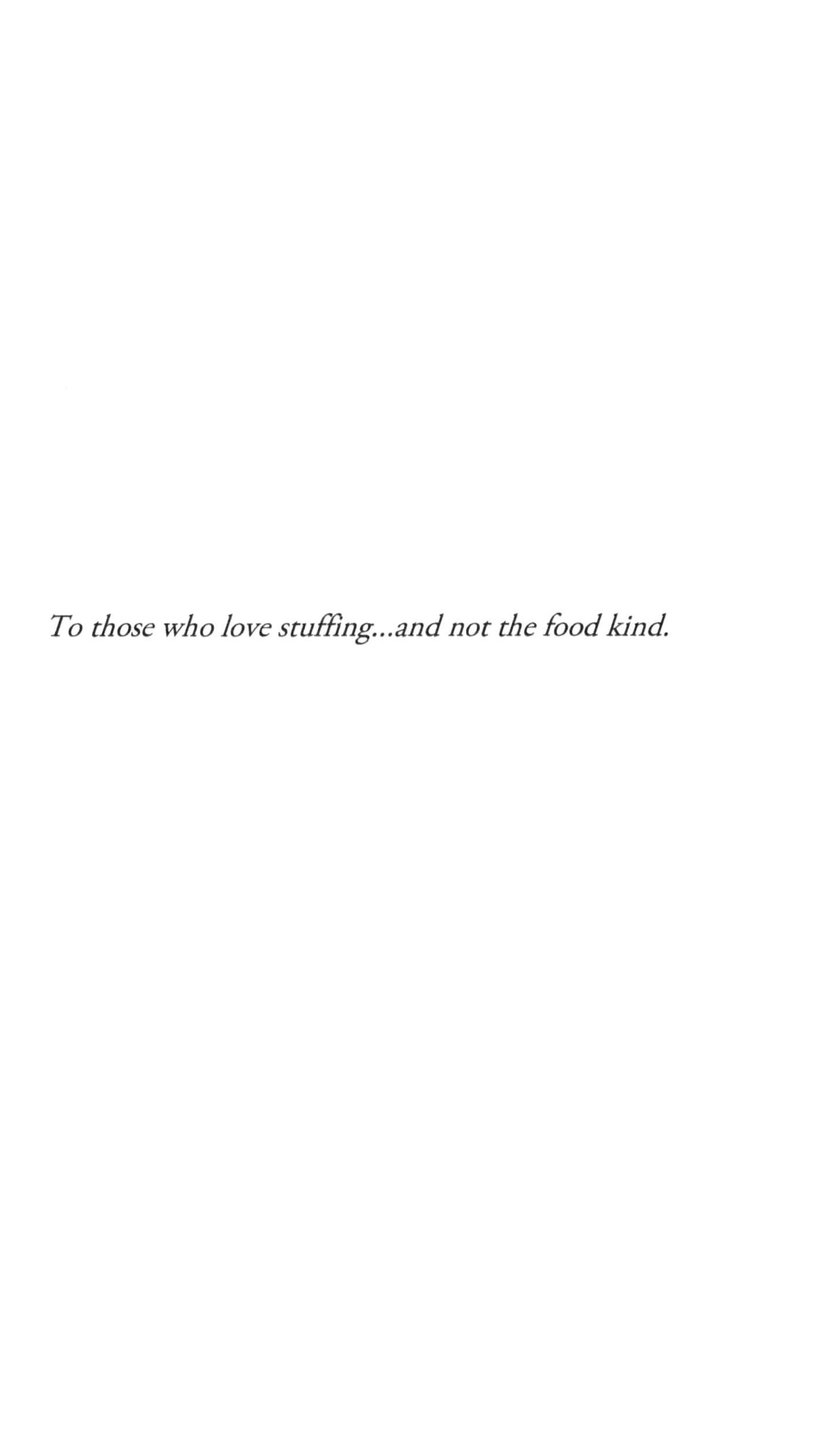

To those who love stuffing...and not the food kind.

LUNAR CREST WINTER

"I'm never going to get this right." Sabina plops onto the ground and pulls her knees to her chest.
Hanging her head, she lets her blond hair, the same
shade as Lyric's, veil her from us.

It takes everything in me not to rush and coddle
her like I want. For one, she'd zap me away, her re-
bellious nature growing more powerful with her age.
Second, I know she needs to learn how to cast her

own magic without my help. It'll help her confidence and enable her to see how bright and amazing her future is. I've never seen anything like Sabina. She pulls her magic from within. She's already surpassed my capabilities at her age.

Sabina sighs. "This is pointless. I'll never be any good. Please just let me go back to my room."

"Don't say that, beanie. You're just as badass and talented as your father. Take a breath and try again," Lyric says, giving Sabina a good shake.

"Your mom's right. You can do this. I know you can." Rubbing my palms together, I summon the spark of magic born from my bond with the most magical woman in existence. "Concentrate on the warmth right in your core and summon it out."

"Please, beanie." Lyric bends down and combs Sabina's hair out of her face to stare our daughter in the eyes.

They are the most beautiful beings I've ever laid eyes on, and I still can't fathom they're my family. My loves. Everything I could've wanted and more. And it doesn't end there. They're like the two suns in my universe and the rest of our pack are the planets. We orbit around our mate and the love born from our bonds, always working together, creating a life we all live equally and blissfully in.

I lean over and rest my hand between Lyric's shoulder blades, using her essence for support as I touch Sabina's chin, getting her to look at us. "I know it's difficult, but the only way you're going to get the hang of it is to keep trying."

"Just let me call it a day. I can't do it," Sabina complains, batting my hand away. "I'm wasting everyone's time."

A familiar howl calls my attention to the trees, picking up my heartbeat. Sterling's presence crashes over me in a wave of warmth, his emotions, desire, and playfulness always as powerful as Lyric's. Sometimes, when we're all together, I can't untangle them or tell the difference. All I know is that we share a bond unlike anything either of us could've ever expected.

"Cut that shit out, mini-blondie. You know you can. You use your power to prank me worse than your dad all the time. Now, get your ass up and spank that magic into obedience. It works on both your parents." Sterling strolls from the edge of the forest in his enchanting wolf form. "Trust me."

Lyric crinkles her nose at me without saying a word. Over the years, we've grown used to Sterling's unfiltered mouth around everyone. And technically, he's not wrong. He's an easy target to fuck with because he's the most easy-going. He can take a prank as good as he pulls them.

"Ew, Uncle," Sabina comments, her face scrunching to mirror Lyric's.

Sabina groans and flicks her fingers at Sterling, sending a burst of lavender light at his paws. Launching off the ground, he pounces on her, catching her off guard. Sterling drags his tongue across her cheek, slobbering on her hair. Sabina hates being pinned as much as Lyric, and it's a sure way to get her to her feet.

"Uncle, you bastard. I don't want that image in my head." Sabina shoves her palms into Sterling's furry chest. "Get off me, or I'm going to blast your ass across Lulupoterra."

Sterling play-growls. "Aw, come on, Niecy. Let me love you. You're never too old for wolf cuddles.

You are the best parts of your parents, and I can't get en—"

"Vo flow nia ba," Sabina chants, managing to grab Sterling's tongue.

He yelps and scrambles off her as lavender magic sparkles over his snout. A strange whimper escapes his mouth, and his long tongue lolls, hanging like a piece of pink meat. Laughing, Lyric bats at Sterling's tongue, swinging it like a pendulum. Sterling shakes his head and bows, trying to touch his tongue with his paws. Sabina takes advantage of his distraction and blasts a bit of power at his hindquarters, sending him onto his back.

"Mercy! I call mercy," Sterling thinks, lying placidly, tucking his tail between his legs.

He whimpers, looking pathetic as fuck, and I can't resist strolling over to tower over him. I grin and stroke my fingers through his chest fur, and he thumps his leg, going from pitiful to cute, and the urge to keep it up courses through me.

Lyric joins me and slides her hand around my back, pulling me closer. Her blue eyes crinkle in the corners with her widening smile. She feels what I do, and if we were alone, this rubdown would turn into something far more satisfying.

"Bested by a teen," Lyric quips, nudging Sterling with her foot, trying to cool us off before things get out of control. Mating season nears in a couple of weeks, which doesn't help. My bond with Lyric makes me feel as out of control as all the mature wolves in Lulupoterra. "You're off your game, old dog. I don't know whether to punish you or cuddle you."

Sterling slurps his tongue over her ankle. "Always both from you, blondie."

"Or neither. It would serve you right for claiming to spank me into submission in front of our daughter, bestie," I think only to him, cocking my eyebrow. "You know you're the one who likes that."

Sterling whimpers again. "I think you need to remind me. It's been hours."

I snort a laugh and shake my head, flicking a bolt of magic at him and rolling him back to his stomach. Sabina dramatically groans and grimaces. She might not hear us, but I'm sure she recognizes our playfulness because we do it so often, especially in front of Lyric. Our beautiful mate loves our bond we have, grown from our love of her, and how we embrace everything she's given to us with each other.

Several howls echo through the air, snagging Sabina's attention. She twists and looks at her brothers, Jett and Jaxson, barreling from the forest in their blond wolf forms with Kian from the Moonlight Canyon pack hot on their trails. He's come to Lunar Crest to hang with Sagan's eldest boys more and more, and while I want to be in denial. I know the truth as to why. The answer sparkles on the young wolf's expression. His ears perk up and he yips in excitement.

Sabina's face lights with what I can only describe as the purest joy at the sight of Harlow and Alonzo's boy, and he slows and cuts away from his friends.

"Dad, Mom. Can we finish this later?" Sabina asks, kneeling down and opening her arms wide in anticipation. "Kian's early, and I don't want him to see how much I suck."

Sterling shakes his head, flinging his tongue

back and forth as it remains heavy and frozen. "Guys like tha—"

Lyric tackles him and cuts off his words, lacing her hands around his muzzle like it'll stop the bastard from thinking. "It's up to your dad."

Sterling thrashes and manages to knock Lyric off, and the two of them start wrestling—Lyric as a woman and Sterling as a wolf. I could watch them mess around like this all day.

Kian stops a dozen feet away and barks, still shy and intimidated by Lyric's presence as a leader. It gets Sterling to give up, letting Lyric pin him while she grins at the young wolf and waves.

"It's nice to see you again, Kian," Lyric says. "Are you looking forward to the games tonight?"

Kian whines and bobs his wolf head before he bows in respect at my beautiful mate. Without having to admit it, Kian already desires a future spot on Sabina's pack, but not only because she's from Lunar Crest. They show signs of a familiar bond, one that won't be fully recognized until maturity. And with knowing that, I suspect Sabina might never transform into a wolf. She's already later than her siblings the same age as her as it is.

"Dad? Please? This is important," Sabina says, drawing my attention away from my thoughts. She tucks her blond hair behind her ears and puckers her bottom lip, taking after her mother with that hard to deny pout.

I tighten my jaw, steeling myself from her oncoming grimace. We both know that it takes a lot in me to deny her request and makes it incredibly hard for me to say no. But one look at Lyric and Sterling tells me if I don't hold firm, I'll be the one bent over and spanked for real...and the thought—I sigh and shove the thought from my mind.

I cross my arms. "I'm sure it is important, but so is this, Sabina. You may go only after you get the spell. I think having Kian here will be helpful. It's always nice to have someone other than your parents cheer you on."

Sabina pops out her bottom lip. "But, Dad."

I hold up my palm. "Try one more time. You've mastered the rain and snow isn't much different. Bring winter to Lunar Crest, so your siblings and uncles can experience the kind of Mortal World

Christmas season I had for years. They've been looking forward to it. We all have."

Sabina glowers at me and flares her nostrils. Raising her hands toward the sky, she gathers lavender magic between her palms. "Wons eci retniw dloc. Go eht vi todo va!"

Kian howls and barks, trotting back and forth in excitement. He feels her energy deep in his bones. I just know it.

Clouds fill the sky with purple lightning bolts, and thunder cracks and booms through the air. The temperature cools until the breath from my mouth fogs, and Lyric snuggles in close to me, shivering. Snow flurries dance through the air, clinging to Sterling's coat and across the ground. Magic buzzes around us as Sabina's spell takes hold of Lunar Crest.

I clap my hands, sending sparks cascading to the ground. "Now this is what I'm talking about. You did it, beanie!"

"Woohoo! That's our girl!" Lyric hops up and down, her tits bouncing in a way that I want to feel on my palms.

I whip my attention to Sterling as he puts his dirty thoughts into my mind. The bastard.

Sabina beams and waves her hands over her head, her blond hair lifting in a blast of freezing wind. "Just wait until I finally shift. I'm going to be the ultimate badass—"

Like the sky explodes, the snow flurries swirl into a storm, turning the world white. Gusting wind whips through Lyric's hair, the whistling noise loud enough to startle Sabina. The world vanishes in a blanket of white, and I can only see a few feet in every direction. Spinning toward me, Sabina stares at me with wide eyes, frozen in shock. She realizes her mistake and looks to me for help. Howls echo through the air with wolf calls, and Dax, Sagan, Bastien, Caz, and Antone bark and call for us from where they stand somewhere within the trees in their wolf forms.

Gathering magic, I shoot it toward the sky with a counter-spell, stopping the blizzard. The snow settles, clearing the air around us and bringing the world back into view. Our pack mates zoom from the trees and circle around us, making sure we're all okay.

Dax transforms into a man, gunning for Lyric like another blizzard might erupt from the sky to carry her away. "What's going on, Flynn? The practice course for the games tonight is getting lost in the snow. We've been out there for—"

Sabina's face falls, her pout turning from me to him. Tears fill her big blue eyes, and she says, "I'm so sorry, Uncle Dax. It was me. I lost control."

Dax freezes under the oncoming girl tears he has no idea what to do with. A dozen thoughts rush through his mind as he internally yells at himself for not thinking. Sighing in defeat, he shoves his thoughts away and palms his forehead. "Little badass, I didn't mean—"

Sabina steps backward as Dax tries to close the space. "No, you're right. I ruined everything. I suck. I can't transform yet and I can't get a spell right. I should just quit and go live in the Mortal World where I belong."

Spinning on her feet, Sabina rushes away and toward the forest instead of the grand housing complex. Lyric sighs and pulls her shirt over her head, preparing to transform. Dax scoops her up and leans in, stopping her.

"Let me talk to her. I messed up." Dax nuzzles his nose to Lyric's.

"You really going to face a teenage witch, Daxy? Look at what happened to my tongue," Sterling says, his words garbled as he stands in his human form with his tongue still hanging out. "She's lucky I can still work with this." He bobs his head up and down. "Sort of."

I tip my head back and laugh, closing the space to him. Cupping his cheeks between my palms, I smile and lean in. With a whisper and a kiss, I counter Sabina's magic with my own until Sterling groans and deepens our kiss, sending desire through me.

"We'll back him up," Bastien says, speaking up from behind me. "It looks like Flynn could use your help, Ma Belle."

"Me fucking too." Sterling pulls away from me. "My ego is bruised, blondie. I need you to kiss and make it feel better."

Lyric kisses Dax once more and shimmies from

his arms. She slips her shirt back on, gaining a collection of groans from our mates. "Okay, horn-dog. But if you stay, you have to help fix the course."

"You bet." Sterling steals Lyric and throws her on his shoulder. "Let those bastards find out what it's like to handle your magical mini."

Sterling transforms with Lyric on his back and trots his way to me. Lyric laughs and clings to his silver coat backwards. Circling me, he stops and licks my hand.

"Come on, warlock. Let's ride him like the majestic beast he is." Lyric grabs my hands, cackling with laughter when I follow through.

Sterling doesn't complain about our weight, his muscular wolf body rippling and flexing with his movements. "I swear if you even consider sinking your sex scepter into her spell cauldron while on my back...I'll be the happiest wolf alive. I want to be the altar you worship her body on."

Reaching behind me, I smack his hindquarters. "If you can get us to the starting line fast enough, you can transform and join us."

Lyric laughs again, hugging me as Sterling takes

off. I lean in and kiss her, tasting the sweetness of her lips against mine. With her closeness, I can forget about the chill of the air around us. Slowing down, Sterling weaves between a few tall trees until we reach a clearing. Lyric eases from my mouth and sucks in a breath in awe.

"Whoa," she whispers. "It's so beautiful."

I help her off Sterling's back. "Like you."

"Smooth, bestie." Stretching his arms over his head, Sterling shows off his muscular body.

Lyric's desire courses through me as she appreciates our mate, loving how sexy he is glistening in the sunlight with water from the melting snow on his heated body. Sauntering to him, Lyric sways her hips and checks him out, giving him her undivided attention. Sterling straightens his shoulders, his bulging muscles flexing. Lyric circles him, running her hands across his pecs and to his biceps, tracing her finger across his shoulder blades and back around to tease his abs. She stands on her tip-toes and slides her arms around his neck, finally stretching to kiss him. Sterling's hard-on slips between her legs with nowhere else to go, and he bounces it, clearly ready to take our mate hard and fast.

So I decide to cool them off.

Flicking my magic at the tree branches overhead, I send snow raining on top of them in a blanket of glistening frost. Lyric squeals and scrambles away, and I summon more magic and knock a pile of snow on top of Sterling up to his waist.

"You naughty warlock," Sterling says, play-growling. "You're in for it now."

Scooping up a handful of snow, Sterling shapes it into a ball. He clomps his way from his snow pile and stalks toward me. I shuffle backward, eyeing the treetops to send more snow onto him.

Sterling jerks his arm, faking me out, and I throw up a magical shield between us. I'm so focused on Sterling that I don't hear Lyric sneaking up on me until it's too late. Plopping a pile of snow on my head, she laughs maniacally and holds me in place. The icy sensation breaks my guard, and I drop my shield. More snow pelts me, melting into my shirt and pants, and I laugh and struggle against my mate as Sterling kicks snow at me in his wolf form.

I shiver and groan as the snow clobbers me. "Aw, come on, bestie. You have a fur coat. I only have a terrible case of shrinkage."

Lyric runs her fingers down my stomach, the heat of her hand like ecstasy, warming my skin. "I can take care of that." Unbuttoning my pants, Lyric slips her hands into my boxers and pulls my hard-on free.

"Shrinkage, my ass. Your cock looks cold resistant." Sterling tip-toes through the snow and opens his arms. "My blue balls are officially ice balls. It's my turn, blondie. Let my stick my icicle into your fire pit. It'll be some amazing sensation play."

Sterling comes up behind Lyric and sandwiches her to me, hugging his arms around the both of us. "All right, warlock. Time for some magic. Preferably warming lube. I'm going in."

Lyric's laughter turns into a moan, and she tightens her hand around my cock, stroking the length of my shaft with enough desperation to get me to turn around. I crash my mouth to hers and kiss her deeply. Sterling's hand hides in her pants and he plays with her clit from behind, making her moan again, the sound so hot that I bet it'll melt the ice around us.

"Toh erif eht eci tlem," I murmur, flicking magic toward the ground.

The snow melts, revealing the soft grass of the clearing. Stripping out of my shirt, I lay it out for Sterling to sit on. He lifts Lyric off her feet and sits down with her between his thighs. I join the two of them, kneeling between their open legs. I'm in the mood to undress our mate, taking my time to savor her sexy body. Instead of magically stealing her clothes, I tug off her athletic pants. She wears nothing under them, sending desire crashing through me. Sterling continues to strum his thumb over her body like he loves playing the delicious melody of her desire.

I kiss the noise from Lyric's mouth, tasting her sweet, soft lips. I could survive on her love and affection—and plan to—because she and my pack makes me feel like the luckiest, most powerful warlock in existence.

Linking my fingers to the hem of her shirt, I

yank it over her head, exposing her tits to the chilly air. I bow into her and flick my tongue on each of her hard nipples, loving the gasp escaping her mouth. Sterling reaches over Lyric's shoulder and runs his fingers through my hair, drawing my attention to him. I lick my way up Lyric's clavicle until I can reach Sterling and kiss him next as Lyric sucks my throat, leaving a mark on my skin. She blindly grabs for me and strokes me with her warm fingers, her body always hotter than mine.

Tensing between us, Lyric moans with her orgasm, sending a shockwave through me. I nip Sterling's bottom lip and stretch it, smiling at him with the pleasure he brings to our mate. We secretly fist-bump over Lyric's shoulder, and I ease back and kiss her again, using magic to lift her body up and onto Sterling's. He growls in satisfaction, enjoying how I bounce her on him, hard and deep until they're panting and gasping with bliss.

Their desire courses through me, and I lower myself onto my elbows and taste Lyric's excitement. Sterling uses two fingers to expose her clit to me, our teamwork to get her off the most natural thing in the world. I suck and lick her while cupping and rubbing Sterling's balls, feeling the tightness of his lust.

"You're teasing me too much," Lyric gasps, her legs trembling. "I need to feel your pleasure too. Any way you want."

"Time to flip over, blondie. I want your mouth on mine." Sterling lies back on the damp grass and turns Lyric over. She rests on top of him with her knees bent, giving me a view of him sliding in and out of her in the slight roughness she enjoys.

I crawl forward on my knees and give her a spank on her ass cheek, loving how her smooth body clenches in anticipation. Her love and excitement wash over me, and she teases me by shaking her hips. She's always been such a giving and attentive lover, ensuring all of our pack mates get what they want and need. I fall more madly in love with her by the second, even after all these years since she first claimed me and accepted part of my soul as her own.

Positioning myself behind her, I summon lube with a spell and take my time dripping it on her.

She pants and gasps, my name on her lips like a screaming plea for the pleasure she knows will come. Even Sterling says my name with her, our bodies linked through our bond, our pleasure as one.

I smile and stroke myself, my muscles rippling as I prepare to slip inside her from behind, completing our circle of passion that will keep me satisfied for days at just the thought. Sterling spreads her ass cheeks for me, and the three of us moan together as I ease in, taking my time to let her body welcome me in. She's so tight and hot, the lube slick and igniting tingles through all my nerve endings.

"My fates, am I in love with you both," I murmur, kissing Lyric's spine as I lose myself to our passion.

"He's so romantic, isn't he?" Sterling murmurs to Lyric, a smile crossing his face.

"Mmmhmm." Lyric's passion consumes her, and I savor her inability to even think coherently.

"Magical. The lord of Pleasuretown," Sterling continues.

I twitch my fingers, sending a shock of magical

vibrations that travel from Lyric to Sterling, bringing them to their peak at the same time. I tip my head back and rock my body through the mind-blowing bliss coursing through me. My balls clench and tighten, and I thrust a few times into Lyric until I cum with a moan.

I slide out of her and lie down, rolling her off Sterling and between us, savoring the heat of her body close to mine. Sunlight trickles through the snowy branches above us, the magic of winter reminding me of the warmth and contentment my pack and my beautiful familiar bring to me. The small misfire of our daughter's spell wasn't a curse but more like a winter miracle. I'm now more determined than ever to show our pack that unexpected surprises bring us things we never knew we wanted or needed, like how I found Lyric in my moment of darkness.

"I hope Sabina realizes what a gift she's given us being the powerful being she is," I murmur, folding my arms over my head.

"I'm sure Dax will ensure it," Lyric says.

"You mean Sagan." Sterling grins and ruffles his

fingers through her damp hair. "Dax is probably running with his tail between his—"

Sterling gasps and growls, none of us hearing Dax's sneak attack. Hooking his paws around Sterling, he humps him playfully. Lyric's loud laugh echoes through the air, and she scrambles up and launches on Dax's back. Howls sound through the air, and I flick my fingers, giving Sterling an advantage by knocking Dax and Lyric off him. Dax transforms into a human, and the three of them roll around the snowy ground, turning it muddy. The rest of our pack mates emerge from the forest to watch what might be the sexiest mud-wrestling match I've ever seen.

A hot arm drapes over my shoulders, and Antone meets my gaze. "Sabina is going to be okay. She is resilient like her mother. Powerful. And with our pack, she will do extraordinary things."

I smile and watch as the others join in on the wrestling match, their love and happiness coursing through me, keeping me warm. "She already does."

A snowball hits me from behind, breaking my thoughts about our pack's future. I spin and catch sight of my coven brother and sisters strolling through the woods, wearing heavy coats. Artemis raises an eyebrow in amusement while Tasha and Sadie dramatically cover their eyes.

"Brother, you're always one with the wolves, aren't you?" Tasha says, twirling her fingers at me. She peeks through her hand. "After all these years, I still can't get used to seeing you as bare as the fates made you coming into this world."

"You would if you'd embrace your wild side, Tash," Sterling says, gathering snow in his hand. "Be one with the woods."

Tasha sends a mound of snow over Sterling's head before he can even raise his arm to retaliate her snowball against me. But she's not fast enough to defend herself from the rest of my pack, turning the wrestling match into a snowball fight.

Antone leaves my side to join the fun, and I laugh and shoot magic into the trees, sending snow drifting over the world. I love seeing everyone laughing and playing around, reminding me of the winters in the Mortal World. But those cold days are nothing in comparison to what my daughter has mistakenly created here. This brilliant winter wolf wonderland is far more magical. It's exactly what we needed.

Cold arms hug me from behind, and I shiver under Lyric's icy embrace. Flipping her over my shoulder with magic, I catch her in my arms and kiss her with every hot, passionate emotion in me, pushing the chill away from both of us. I whisper a spell under my breath and summon a blanket, draping it around our bodies.

I ease away and grin, loving how perfect this moment feels. "I still sometimes can't believe how lucky I am, she-wolf. My perfect mate. Perfect pack. All of our beautiful children and family."

"You forgot our perfect love and world," she muses, snuggling close. "There is only one thing missing."

"What's that?" I ask.

"The mistletoe!" Sterling shouts, shaking snow from his light hair.

Lyric laughs. "And the lights."

"You know, Ma Belle," Bastien says, strolling up to us. He sandwiches Lyric between us, and I use magic to extend the blanket to cover him too, "we shouldn't change anything for the games. No new course. No fixing the old one. Let's just gather the packs and run."

Light sparkles in Lyric's eyes, her gaze reflecting the magic in mine. "I love the sound of that. Let's gather everyone. Tonight will start a new tradition in Lulupoterra. Instead of the Pack-Mate Games all season, we will also include the Winter Wolf Games."

Sterling joins our blanket hug, sliding close to me and Lyric. "With snow, lights, mistletoe—"

"Lots of blankets and maybe the finish line leading to a hot spring," Dax says, cutting him off. He messes up Sterling's hair and kisses Lyric's temple.

Sagan, Caz, and Antone join us, and Sagan says, "Let's call everyone now."

They all howl in unison in their human forms, and I join along with them, laughing and hugging and loving up on my pack.

With a flick of my fingers, I shoot magic into the sky, setting the world aglow. "Let the Winter

Wolf Games begin!"

"Come on, Sabina. Run with us," Aria calls, waving her hand at Sabina. She ties her platinum hair into a ponytail and shivers. I love how close Sterling's daughter is with ours.

I huddle between Sterling and Lyric, watching our children prepare for the games. Hundreds of wolves from all over Lulupoterra howl and play in the snow. I don't think I've seen the younger pups have so much fun. They're usually far more intense, letting their competitive sides consume them.

"Yeah, Sabina-Bina. You can ride me." Kian jerks his attention in our direction. His face flushes with Sterling's cackling laughter at the teen's unintentional innuendo.

Sabina twists and tries to spell Sterling, but I block her with a shield.

Sterling gives her a cocky-bastard smile. I know he can't help himself when he finds something funny. "Aw, Niecy. You have to admit it was hilarious. If your puppy-love can't handle a little joking, he doesn't deserve—"

I drop the shield, and Sabina spells his tongue again, stopping him from speaking.

"Uncle, knock it off. It's not like that." Sabina narrows her eyes and glares.

"Yet." Sterling shakes his head, trying to unfreeze his tongue.

She groans and twists, jogging toward Aria and Kian with a few of Kian's brothers. I offer her a smile and a nod of encouragement. Lyric slides her fingers through mine and gives me a squeeze, her mind playing the same thoughts as me about Sabina's future with the packs.

"Stop worrying, you two. Sabina will find her place just as you both have," Sterling says, his words coming out garbled.

I lean in and kiss him, countering Sabina's spell. "You're right."

"What's my reward for that?" he teases.

"A spot on my naughty list." Lyric beams him a smile and smacks his ass hard enough to make him jump and groan. "Punishment will come however you'd like."

"Add me to the list, gorgeous," Sagan says, wagging his brows.

The whistle indicating the start of the games sounds through the air and our pack mates gather around us to face the rest of the wolf packs of Lulupoterra. Excitement and joy buzzes through the air, and I rub my hands together. Throwing my arms above my head, I send magic through the forest, illuminating Lunar Crest with millions of rainbow lights, turning the white night forest festive. The packs cheer and bounce on their feet in anticipation as they wait for Lyric to make her announcement.

She steps forward, her shoulders straight and her head held high. "It is a great honor to start a new tradition in Lulupoterra. I mark today as the beginning of the Winter Wolf Games that will test our strengths and help bond us as a community. With our love and power, our families and friends, may we remember that as long as we're together, we will always find warmth when the world feels cold."

The starting whistle cuts through the night, and everyone cheers and transforms into their wolf forms. Lyric spins and throws her arms around me, silently begging me to lift her up. The rest of our pack surrounds us, hugging and laughing, watching as the wolves take off into the night.

I never in my existence imagined that this is how my world would be—with the Lunar Crest pack, our children, powerful magic, and endless love and devotion—and I couldn't be any more grateful. Not only is the woman I love the most magical being I've ever met, she also embodies the true spirit of the holidays, so full of bliss, happiness, and everything good in the universe I can survive on forever.

Laughter draws my attention from Lyric and to our pack, and I shake my head at the snowman the guys build. The rainbow lights cast a magical glow. Snow flurries drift through the air, illuminating the world with dazzling color. I rub my hands on Lyric's arms, pushing away the cold.

"Snow-Dax is complete," Sterling says, chuckling.

"Not quite big enough." Dax crosses his arms, staring at the snow-cock Sterling added.

Tipping her head back, Lyric laughs and dashes

over to them. She gets on her knees and inspects it, lacing her fingers around the bulge. "You're right. I can easily fit my mouth around this popsicle without stretching my jaw."

"Careful what you say. You're turning us all on, blondie. My cocksicle is so cold I might get stuck in your wet wonderland." Sterling strokes himself.

"I'm willing to try. The worst that can happen is I get to make love to our mate for the rest of the games. Ensure some new additions. Maybe we'll finally have our little girl," Dax murmurs, scooping Lyric up.

She pats his chest and leans in to kiss him. "It's not even mating season yet."

"I thought no babies this year. If that's the case, sign me up, gorgeous. I miss the baby snuggles," Sagan says.

Lyric loves the sound of it. I can feel it in my very essence. "You guys make it so hard to resist."

"Because you make us hard," Dax teases.

A whistle cuts through the air as the first wolves already cross the finish line.

Bastien claps his hands and rubs them together.

"All right, Ma Belle. Time to run. You better hurry or I'll give you a nip."

"Me first." Antone transforms into a wolf and stalks toward Lyric.

She squeals and dashes away into the trees, getting our pack riled up already. They love a good game of chase. Caz collides into Antone, knocking him out of the way. Sagan and Bastien playfully wrestle Dax. Lyric's familiar howl sounds through the air, grabbing their attention, and the five wolves bolt after her.

"All right, bestie. Ready to go?" Sterling asks, resting his hands on my shoulders. "I have a surprise for our beautiful blondie and want to beat them to the finish line."

I turn around and tilt my head, following his pointing finger down his naked body. I clutch my gut and bellow with uncontrollable laughter at Sterling's attempt to make it look as if mistletoe hangs from his hard-on using some leaves.

"Here, let me help you," I say, whispering a spell under my breath.

Sterling inhales a breath of a moan at the sensation of my magic lacing around his boner as I tie a ribbon with real mistletoe onto his cock. He flexes, listening to the jingle of golden bells dangling down. I can't stop laughing.

"So...how does this work? We're above the mistletoe. Maybe you can get lower and really give me some holiday magic," Sterling murmurs, stepping closer.

I cock an eyebrow and cup his cheek in my hand. "Is that your Christmas wish?"

Leaning in, he brushes his lips to mine. "Along with a few other things."

"Like what?" My body hardens at his lust pouring into me, the night of our winter romp with Lyric fresh in our minds.

"Like me on my knees beside you," Lyric says, leaning against a tree, her body glistening and wet with the fresh snow. "Maybe in our den with the others."

"That sounds perfect, blondie. The best gift ever." Sterling extends his hand to her, getting her to saunter closer.

She snuggles between us, letting us press flush

against her icy body. "Maybe I'll even grant you what you've been dying to try."

Sterling play-growls. "Don't joke. My blue balls will never recover if you are."

I shake my head. "Well, you are on the naughty list."

Sterling leans over her shoulder and gets in close. "So are you if you don't hurry. If you want your wand to join my rocket in her Christmas cookie, let's go."

Groaning, Lyric hops in my arms and presses her cool lips to my earlobe. "I hope you can grant me a little magical miracle for this adventure. I might need it. Maybe help me stretch."

"Don't worry, blondie. You're used to Dax," Sterling teases.

She laughs, filling my heart and soul with her love, light, and pure enchanting magic.

Waving my hand, I cast sparkling light through the air, raining magic through the world. "This will be the most memorable Winter Wolf Games. I promise."

Sterling holds on tightly to us as I transport us

into our den. Warm air engulfs us, and the rest of our pack mates smile at us from their places warming up in the hot spring.

"Hell yeah, it will be, blondie," Sterling says, stealing her away from me. "I hope you're hungry for our affection."

"Starving." Lyric bites her lip and teases our pack mates by touching between her legs.

Moaning, Sterling kisses her. "Good, because you're about to get stuffed."

-The End-

Thank you so much for reading *Winter Wolf Games, The Pack Mates of Lunar Crest Short Story*! I hope you enjoyed this magical adventure. It was great celebrating winter in Lunar Crest. May your holidays be warm, bright, and magical.

I HOPE YOU LOVED A glimpse of Lunar Crest fifteen years after The Witch Chase! To stay up-to-date with future The Pack Mates of Lunar Crest stories and books featuring the pack's next generation, make sure to follow Ginna online and join her Facebook Group: Paranormal Center for Matches and Mates.

Other Reverse Harem Novels by Ginna Moran

THE VAMPIRE HEIRS WORLD

The Divine Vampire Heirs
Blood Match

Blood Rebel

Blood Debt

Blood Feud

Blood Loss

Blood Vows*

The Royale Vampire Heirs Series:
Rebel Vampires

Rebel Dhampir

Rebel Match

Rebel Heir

Rebel Fight

Academy of Vampire Heirs Series:
Dhampirs 101

Blood Sources 102

Coven Bonds 103

Personal Donors 104

Blood Wars 105

THE MATES OF MAGAELORUM WORLD

The Pack Mates of Lunar Crest:

The She-Wolf Games

The Wolf-Mate Trials

The Omega Hunt

The Witch Chase

The Inmate of the Dreki Dragons:

Maximum Magical Penitentiary: Falsely Accused

Maximum Magical Penitentiary: Deadly Fugitive

Maximum Magical Penitentiary: Death Row

THE SEVEN SINNERS
OF HELL'S KINGDOM

Her Personal Demons

Her Deadly Angels

THIS BOOK WOULDN'T HAVE EVER come to be without the organizers of the holiday collection entitled All the Festive Bits. Thanks for inviting me to join such a fun project!

GINNA MORAN IS the author of over fifty novels including the popular The Pack Mates of Lunar Crest, The Seven Sinners of Hell's Kingdom, Academy of Vampire Heirs, The Divine Vampire Heirs, and The Royale Vampire Heirs WhyChoose novels.

She always carried a fascination for all things paranormal and wrote her first unpublished manuscript at age eighteen. Her love of the supernatural grew stronger through her adult life, and she now spends her days with different creatures of the night. Whether it's vampires, werewolves, dragons, fae, angels, demons, or mermaids, Ginna loves creating and living in worlds from her dreams.

Aside from Ginna's professional life, she enjoys binge watching TV, crafting and design, playing pretend with her daughter, and cuddling with her dogs. Some of her favorite things include chocolate, mermaids, anything that glitters, learning new things, cheesy jokes, and organizing her bookshelf.

Ginna is currently hard at work on her next novel and the one after, and the one after that.